THE
North Carolina
Alphabet

T0151348

by
Pamela
George
and
Walter
Brown

Carolina Wren Press

Copyright 2005 Pamela George and Walter M. Brown

The mission of Carolina Wren Press is to seek out, nurture
and promote literary work by new and underrepresented
writers, including women and writers of color.

Design: Lesley Landis Designs

This publication was made possible in part by a generous
grant from The Mary Duke Biddle Foundation. In addition, we gratefully
acknowledge the ongoing support made possible through gifts
to the Durham Arts Council's United Arts Fund
and from the North Carolina Arts Council.

Library of Congress
Cataloging-in-Publication Data

George, Pamela.
The North Carolina Alphabet
by Pamela George and Walter M. Brown.
p. cm.
ISBN 0-932112-50-1 (alk. paper)
1. North Carolina—Juvenile literature.
2. English language—Alphabet—
Juvenile literature. I. Brown, Walter M.,
1927- II. Title.

F254.3.G46 2005
975.6—dc22

2005021898

THE North Carolina Alphabet

by
Pamela
George
and
Walter
Brown

Carolina Wren Press

A is for Alligator ...

B is for Beaver...

C is for Cardinal...

D is for Dogs...

E is for Eagle...

F is for Frogs...

G is for Garden...

H is for Heron...

I is for Iris...

J is for Jellyfish...

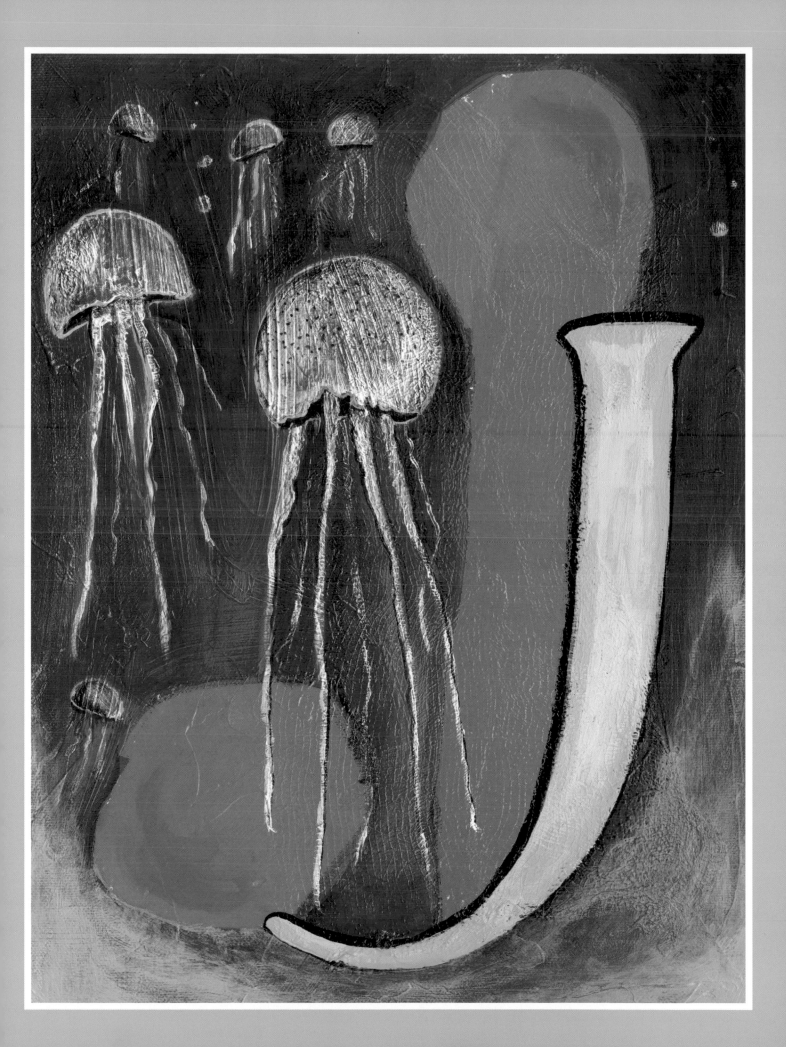

K is for Kites...

L is for Lighthouse...

M is for Mountains...

N is for Nest...

O is for Opossum...

P is for Pig...

Q is for Queen Anne's Lace...

R is for Raccoon...

S is for Seashells...

T is for Tobacco
farm...

U is for Umbrella...

V is for Venus flytrap...

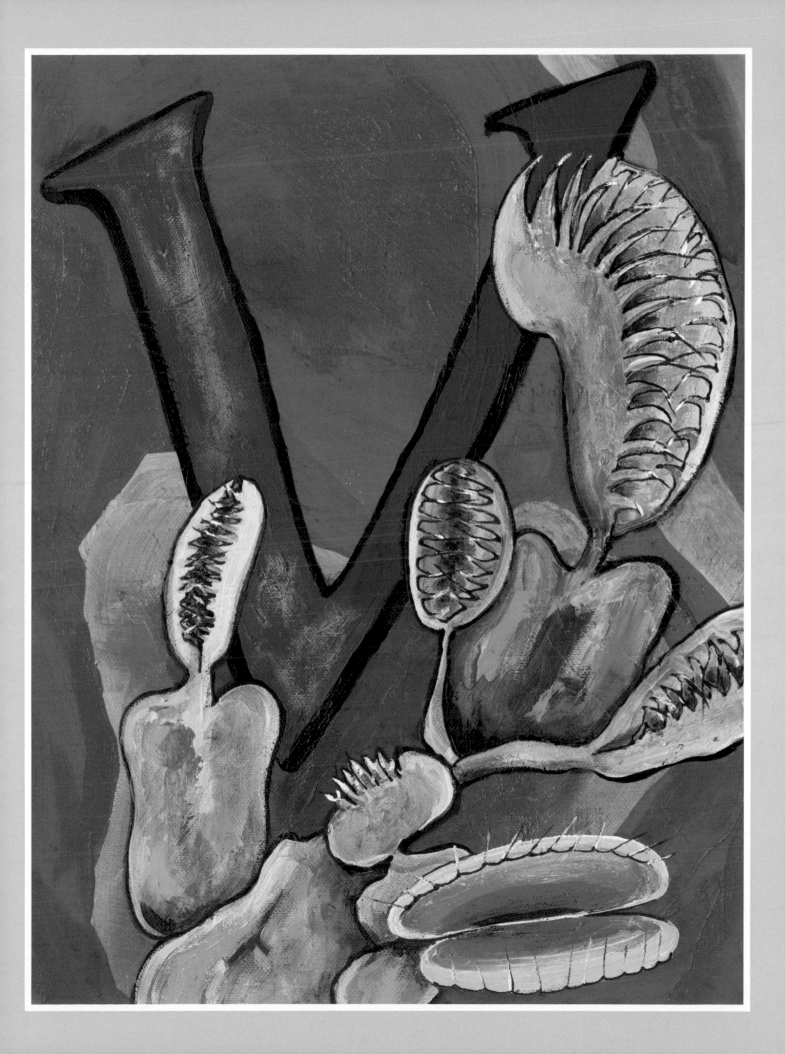

W is for Woodpecker...

X is for Fox...

Y is for Yellowjackets...

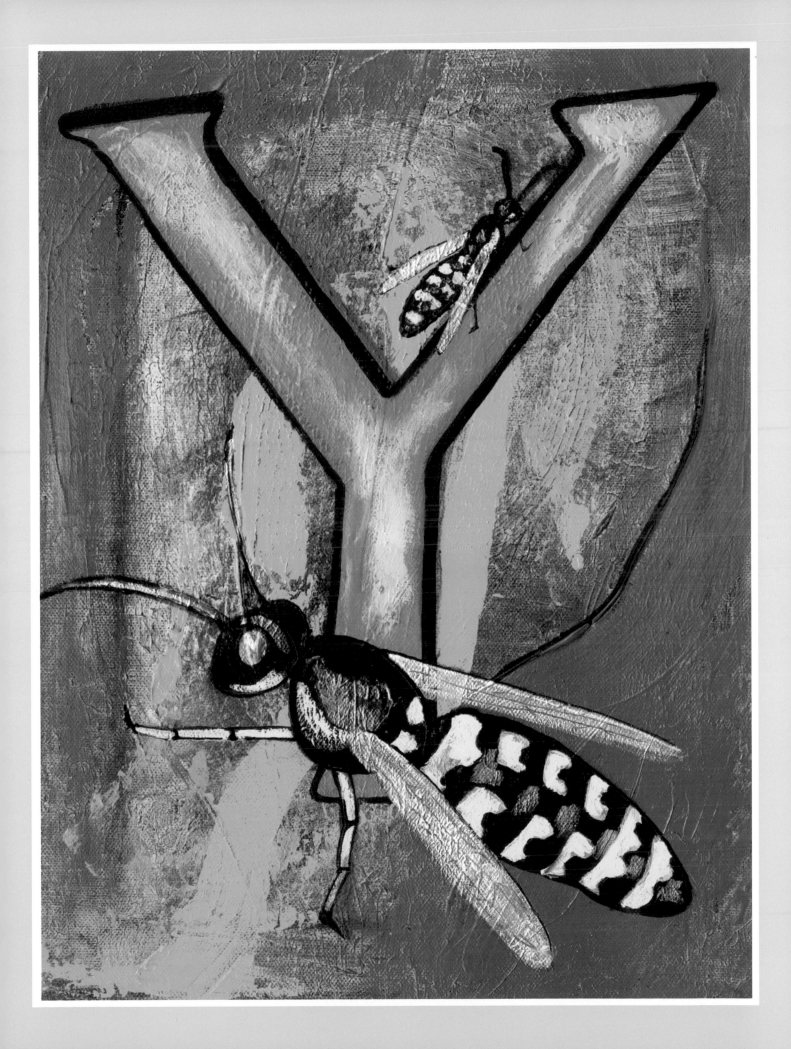

Z is for Zoo...

The North Carolina Alphabet

Teachers and students helped us by offering possible words and images for this alphabet. It was very difficult to choose the best ones among their good suggestions. First, we decided to pick words and pictures that represented North Carolina outdoor life from the mountains to the coast. We then chose words that were easy to remember, but still had some elements for discovery. Finally, we wanted to draw and paint images that were from both exotic and everyday life in our state. If you were making a state alphabet, which words would you choose?

A Alligator, acorn, aquarium, airplane, ant, Appalachia, apple

B Beaver, bat, barn, beach, bear, bee, bluebird, Blue Ridge, boat, bobcat, bream, buoy

C Cardinal, Carolina wren, catfish, cliff, compost, copperhead, cotton, cow, crab, crayfish

D Dogs, deer, dogwood, dolphin, dove, dragonfly, duck, dune

E Eagle, ebb tide, eel, egret, emerald, estuary

F Frogs, farm, fern, Ferris wheel, fig, firefly, fish, fleas, flight, flounder, flying squirrel, fog

G Garden, gardenia, garter snake, gems, ghost, goat, goose, gorge, gypsy moth

H Heron, harbor, hawksbill, hemlock, hills, honey, horseshoe crab, huckleberry, hurricane

I Iris, ice, inlet, inner tubes, island, ivy

J Jellyfish, jack-in-the-pulpit, jay, jetty, June bug

K Kites, kayak, kingfisher, kitten, kudzu

L Lighthouse, ladybug, lady slipper, laurel, lichen, lily pads, loggerhead, loon

M Mountains, magnolia, mica, mole, monarch butterfly, mosquito, mushroom

N Nest, newt, nettle, nut tree

O Opossum, oak tree, otter, outer banks, owl, oyster

P Pig, pelican, pickle, piedmont, pier, pine tree, pitcher plant, poplar, pumpkin

Q Queen Anne's Lace, quagmire, quail, quarry, quartz

R Raccoon, rabbit, ram, rattlesnake, river, roach, road kill, rocks, rooster

S Seashells, salamander, sand, seagull, shark, shrimp, snake, snow, spider, surf, swan

T Tobacco farm, tern, terrapin, ticks, timber, toad, topsail, trout, tulip tree, turkey, turtle

U Umbrella, under water, up-and-down

V Venus flytrap, valley, vegetables, vines, viper, vireo

W Woodpecker, waders, warbler, waterspout, waves, whelk, whitetail, wolf

X Fox, ax, box kite, "X marks the spot"

Y Yellow jackets, yacht, yam, yawl

Z Zoo, zinnias

Y IDEA FOR A NORTH CAROLINA ALPHABET WAS BORN OUT OF THREE devotions—kids, geography and painting. First, when I was a beginning special education teacher more than three decades ago, some of the students I was teaching had not yet learned to read, even though they were in middle school. Few interesting, attractive materials were available for them. So one of my first successful projects was to design a set of colorful, textural letters using images they suggested. Later, in Samoa in the South Pacific as a Peace Corps volunteer, I was teaching geography and had to use a book in which the map of Samoa fell into the book's gutter—not to be seen at all. We had to construct our own maps if geography class was going to make sense. These teaching experiences convinced me that learning materials work best when they are relevant to students' lives.

Second, North Carolina doesn't have its own alphabet. Vermont has a wonderful "Farmer's Alphabet" by Mary Azarian, which can be seen in almost every classroom with that state's young readers. Our North Carolina "M" shows the beautiful Blue Ridge mountains and is intentionally different than the Vermont "M" depicting maple syrup. This difference teaches regional diversity as well as the letter "M." I wanted *The North Carolina Alphabet* to honor our state's extraordinary natural resources and rich rural heritage without being quaint.

Third, as an artist, I love to paint animals and landscapes. Each letter, in its original design, is a large acrylic painting on canvas full of texture, botanical collage material and light. Walter Brown's exquisite letters danced right onto the canvases. The pure cool and warm colors are ones young children would likely choose, but the complex textures allow layers of color to peek through.

Many people helped with this alphabet. Ryan Erwin and Lauren Friedman, wonderful young artists themselves, helped me as studio assistants. Many professors and students of the North Carolina Central School of Education offered ideas for words and imagery representative of North Carolina outdoor life. Judy May, Charlotte Wilson and Lisa Kempf are my constant advisors and the kind of exemplary teachers I am proud to know. Kirsten Mullen and Linda McGloin of the North Carolina Arts Council encouraged me in this project's many possibilities. Jane Filer, a North Carolina artistic treasure, provided me excellent example as a master painter. Kemen, David and JamJam Austin were my constant buoys. With these helpers and Walter Brown's calligraphy, *The North Carolina Alphabet* took flight.

—Pamela George

INCE THE 1950s, I HAVE HAD A SUSTAINING INTEREST IN THE ARTISTRY
of hand-lettered documents before Gutenberg, and my interest in calligraphy started when I took a beginning course at Montgomery County (Maryland) Community College in 1970. Later, Patsy Crouch, one of the Washington, D.C., metropolitan area's most accomplished calligraphers, took me on as a tutee. Since I studied with Patsy and a number of visiting letter artists, mainly European, calligraphy became for me a consuming passion.

Pamela George and I were faculty colleagues in the School of Education at North Carolina Central University. She was acquainted with my practice in calligraphy, having received holiday greeting cards that I designed over consecutive years. I saw the brilliance of her artistic talents when I attended her first painting exhibition, and when she extended the opportunity to do the calligraphy for *The North Carolina Alphabet*, my acceptance was immediate and enthusiastic. The outcome of this team effort is a major artistic milestone for both of us.

—Walter Brown